For Italy . . . her art, her music and her people.
—CF

For Valentina, Laura and Siu
—OS

First published in the UK in 2020
by New Frontier Publishing Europe Ltd
Uncommon, 126 New King's Road, London, SW6 4LZ
www.newfrontierpublishing.co.uk

ISBN: 978-1-912858-59-0

A CIP catalogue record for this book
is available from the British Library.

Designed by Celeste Hulme

Printed in China
10 9 8 7 6 5 4 3 2 1

One Lone Swallow

Corinne Fenton

Illustrated by Owen Swan

NEW FRONTIER PUBLISHING

Florence, Italy,

around 1805, at twilight

As the bells of Florence called to one another
above the ancient walls and towers,

one lone swallow flew.

As the moon peeped from behind
softly blown night-clouds,
then lingered above the chimney-tops
and ruffled roofs,
one lone swallow flew.

As candles blinked from shuttered windows
and giant filmy cobwebs danced in the twilight breeze,
one lone swallow flew, searching.

Always at dusk she flew this way,
sure and swift.
But this night was different.

This night she was
searching for her mate,
and her nestlings were left all alone.

'Witt-witt,' she cried.

She flew with grace and speed,
flitting and darting, writing music with her wings,
over the churches,

under the bridges,

through the arches

and above the city's piazzas.

Over the highest belltower she searched,

above each rooftop

along the wide river,

and beyond the charcoal edges
of the ancient city,

but she could not find him.

For a moment she rested
and gazed down upon the whole city –
over each belltower,
along each winding road
and across to the Tuscan hills.
'Witt-witt,' she cried.
She knew she must hurry –
her nestlings would be waiting,
hungry,
calling.

She watched as flocks of pigeons swept like silvery beams
over the old city,
but she could not find her mate.

Then, far away,
at the feet of the most treasured statue,
her keen eyes caught a flicker, a flutter.

She flew as fast as a hunter's arrow
and there she found him,

one wing tangled in shoemakers' twine.
'Splee-plink,' he cried.

And while the bells of Florence called to one another,
as the moon peeped from behind softly blown night-clouds,
then lingered above the chimney-tops and ruffled roofs,

the mother swallow hovered,
tugging and pulling,

flying backwards and forwards
many times …
gently unravelling the tangled threads
from her mate's captured wing –
tugging and pulling,
holding steady.

She was so intent upon her task
that at first she did not notice the giant house rat

scuttling

ever closer.

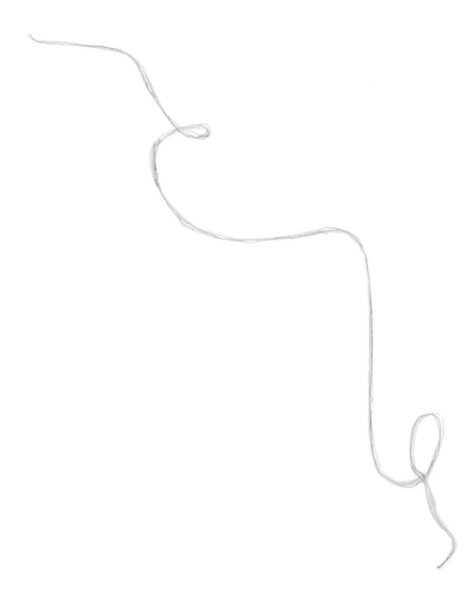

Then, in the hold-a-breath moment
before the rat-menace scurried forward
to its prey,
the final thread fell loose.

As a blue velvet night draped whispers
over the timeless city
and the bells fell silent
above the ancient walls and towers,
two swallows flew home …

to their nestlings.